N
LIGHTS
for *Moms*

New Leaf Press

First Printing: March 2004

Cover and Interior design by Brent Spurlock
Edited by Jim Fletcher and Roger Howerton

ISBN: 0-89221-570-4
Library of Congress Catalog Card Number:
2003116015

Please visit our web site for more great titles:
www.newleafpress.net

New Leaf Press

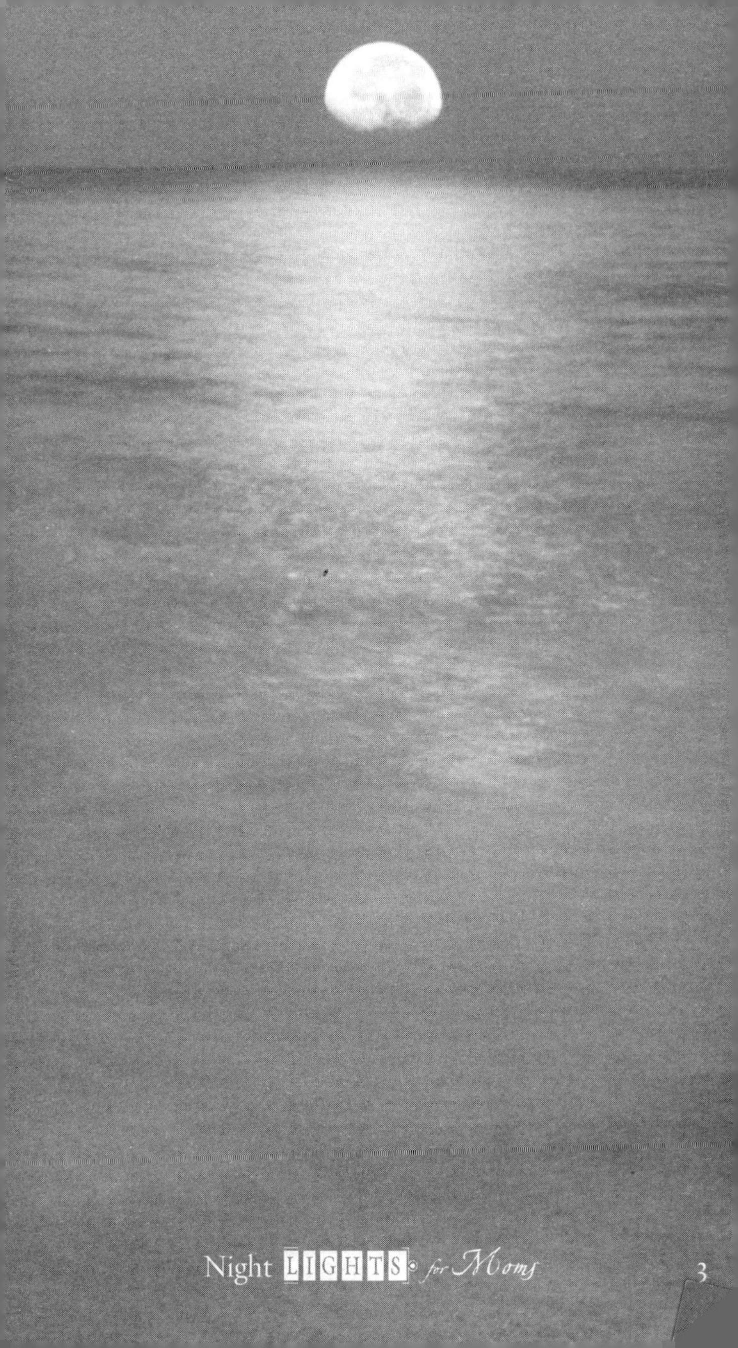

A special gift for you

To

_____

From

_____

A MOM'S VERSION OF
FIRST CORINTHIANS 13

If I live in a house of spotless beauty with everything in its place, but have not love, I am a housekeeper – not a homemaker.

If I have time for waxing, polishing and decorative achievements, but have not love, my children learn of cleanliness – not godliness.

Love leaves the dust in search of a child's laugh.

Love smiles at the tiny fingerprints on a newly cleaned window.

Love wipes away the tears before it wipes up the spilled milk.

Love picks up the child before it picks up the toys.

Love is present through the trials.

Love reprimands, reproves, and is responsive.

Love crawls with the baby, walks with the toddler, runs with the child, then stands aside to let the youth walk into adulthood.

Love is the key that opens salvation's message to a child's heart.

Before I became a mother I took glory in my house of perfection.

Now I glory in God's perfection of my child.

As a mother there is much I must teach my child, but the greatest of all is love.

TODAY ...

TOMORROW ...

Write down your thoughts, dreams, and hopes.

> So faith, hope, love abide, these three; but
> the greatest of these is love.
> — 1 Corinthians 13:13 (RSV)

Youth fades; love droops;

the leaves of friendship fall;

A mother's secret love

outlives them all.

- Oliver Wendell Holmes

REFLECTING ON CHARACTER

The light turns green, but the man doesn't notice. The woman, in a convertible, waits, but the man doesn't notice the light change. The woman begins pounding on her steering wheel and yelling at the man to move.

The man doesn't move. The woman is going ballistic inside her car, ranting and raving at the man, pounding on her steering wheel and dash. The light turns yellow. The woman begins to blow the car horn and scream curses at the man.

The man, hearing the commotion, looks up, sees the yellow light and accelerates through the intersection just as the light turns red. The woman is beside herself, screaming in frustration as she misses her chance to get through the intersection.

As she is still in mid-rant she looks up into the barrel of a gun held by a very serious looking policeman. The policeman tells her to shut off her car while keeping both hands in sight. She complies, speechless at what is happening. After she shuts off the engine, the policeman orders her to exit her car with her hands up. She gets out of the car and he orders her to turn and place her hands on her car. She turns, places her hands on the car and quickly is cuffed and hustled into the patrol car. She is too bewildered by the chain of events to ask any questions and is driven to the police station where she is fingerprinted, photographed, searched, booked and placed in a cell.

After a couple of hours, a policeman approaches the cell and opens the door for her. She is escorted back to the booking desk where the original officer is waiting with her personal effects. He hands her the bag containing her things, and says, "I'm really sorry for this mistake. But you see, I pulled up behind your car while you were blowing your horn and cussing a blue streak at the car in front of you and then I noticed the 'Choose Life' license plate holder and the 'Follow Me to Sunday School' bumper sticker and the chrome-plated Christian fish emblem on the trunk, so naturally I assumed you had stolen the car."

$\mathbf{T}$ODAY ...

$\mathbf{T}$OMORROW ...

Write down your thoughts, dreams, and hopes.

Now then we are ambassadors for Christ....
— 2 Corinthians 5:20

Christian action is not of

ourselves; it is the spirit of Christ

operating in our lives.

— Anonymous

SIGNS OF A HAPPY HOME

Here are some sayings from those little hand-painted signs that hang in so many kitchens:

A messy kitchen is a happy kitchen and this kitchen is delirious.

No husband has ever been shot while doing the dishes.

A husband is someone who takes out the trash and gives the impression he just cleaned the whole house.

If we are what we eat, then I'm fast, cheap, and easy.

A balanced diet is a cookie in each hand.

Thou shalt not weigh more than thy refrigerator.

Blessed are they who can laugh at themselves for they shall never cease to be amused.

A clean house is a sign of a misspent life.

Help keep the kitchen clean — eat out.

Housework done properly can kill you.

Countless numbers of people have eaten in this
    kitchen and gone on to lead normal lives.

My next house will have no kitchen —
    just vending machines.

The only reason I have a kitchen is because it
    came with the house when I bought it.

There are only three kinds of food: frozen,
    canned, and take-out!

TODAY...

TOMORROW...

Write down your thoughts, dreams, and hopes.

> Unless the LORD builds the house, those
> who build it labor in vain.
>
> – Psalm 127:1

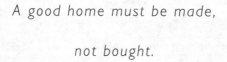

A good home must be made,

not bought.

– Joyce Maynard

A PRAYER OF ST. FRANCIS

Lord, make me an instrument of Thy peace.
Where there is hatred, let me sow love;
Where there is injury, pardon;
Where there is doubt, faith;
Where there is despair, hope;
Where there is darkness, light;
Where there is sadness, joy.

Divine Master,
Grant that I may not so much seek to be
    consoled as to console;
To be understood as to understand;
To be loved as to love;
For it is in giving that we receive;
It is in pardoning that we are pardoned;
It is in dying that we are born
Unto eternal life.

If we are afflicted, it is for your comfort and salvation; and if we are comforted, it is for your comfort, which you experience when you patiently endure the same sufferings that we suffer.
– 2 Corinthians 1:6 (RSV)

TODAY ...

TOMORROW ...

Write down your thoughts, dreams, and hopes.

THREE WISE WOMEN

You do know what would have happened if it had been three wise WOMEN from the East instead of men, don't you? They would have asked for directions, arrived on time, helped deliver the baby, cleaned the stable, made a casserole and brought disposable diapers as gifts!

My mouth shall speak of wisdom; and the meditation of my heart shall be of understanding.

– Psalm 49:3

TODAY ...

_____
_____
_____
_____
_____
_____
_____
_____
_____
_____

TOMORROW ...

_____
_____
_____
_____

Write down your thoughts, dreams, and hopes.

White **LIES**

ormer president Jimmy Carter spoke at Southern Methodist University and related an incident that occurred after he left the White House. A woman reporter came to Plains, Georgia, to interview his mother in relation to an article about Mr. Carter and his family. His mother really didn't want to be interviewed, but was being gracious. So when the reporter knocked at her door, Mrs. Carter invited her in. The reporter asked some hard questions and actually was rather aggressive and rude.

"I want to ask you a question," she said. "Your son ran for the presidency on the premise that he would always tell the truth. Has he ever lied?"

Mrs. Carter said, "I think he's truthful; I think you can depend on his word."

The reporter again asked if he had ever lied in his entire life.

His mother said, "Well, I guess maybe he's told a little white lie."

"Ah, see there!" the reporter exclaimed. "He's lied! If he told a white lie, he has lied."

The reporter was still not satisfied and asked, "What is a white lie?"

And then Lillian Carter said, "It's like a moment ago when you knocked on the door and I went to the door and said I was glad to see you."

TODAY ...

_____

_____

_____

_____

_____

_____

_____

_____

_____

_____

TOMORROW ...

_____

_____

_____

_____

_____

Write down your thoughts, dreams, and hopes.

... he began to say to his disciples first,
"Beware of the leaven of the Pharisees,
which is hypocrisy.

– Luke 12:1

A half truth is a whole lie.

– Yiddish proverb

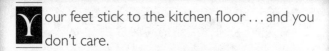

Your feet stick to the kitchen floor ... and you don't care.

The kids are fighting, and you threaten to lock them in a room together and not let them out until someone's bleeding.

You can't find your cordless phone, so you ask a friend to call you, and you run around the house madly, following the sound until you locate the phone downstairs in the laundry basket.

You spend an entire week wearing sweats.

Popsicles become a food staple.

Your favorite television show is a cartoon.

Peanut butter and jelly is eaten in at least one meal a day.

Your baby's pacifier falls on the floor and you give it back to her after you suck the dirt off of it because you're too busy to wash it off.

You're so desperate for adult conversation that you spill your guts to the telemarketer that calls and HE hangs up on YOU!

Spit is your number one cleaning agent.

You buy cereal with marshmallows in it.

You count the sprinkles on each kid's cupcake to make sure they're equal.

You have time to shave only one leg at a time.

You hide in the bathroom to be alone.

You think finger paint should be a controlled substance.

You've mastered the art of placing food on a plate without anything touching.

You hire a sitter because you haven't been out with your husband in ages, then spend half the night talking about and checking on the kids.

You hope ketchup is a vegetable because it's the only one your child eats.

You fast-forward through the scene when the hunter shoots Bambi's mother.

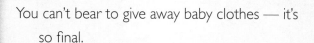

You can't bear to give away baby clothes — it's
  so final.

You read that the average five year old asks 437
  questions a day and feel proud that your kid
  is "above average."

You say at least once a day, "I'm not cut out for
  this job," but you know you wouldn't trade it
  for anything.

TODAY ...

TOMORROW ...

Write down your thoughts, dreams, and hopes.

> Let your father and mother be glad, let her
> who bore you rejoice.
>
> – Proverbs 23:25

Motherhood is the greatest

privilege of life.

– *May R. Coker*

The SILVERSMITH

S ome time ago, a few ladies met to study the Scriptures. While reading the third chapter of Malachi, they came upon a remarkable expression in the third verse. "And He shall sit as a refiner and purifier of silver" (Malachi 3:3).

One lady decided to visit a silversmith, and report to the others on what he said about the subject. She went accordingly, and without telling him the reason for her visit, begged the silversmith to tell her about the process of refining silver. After he had fully described it to her, she asked, "Sir, do you sit while the work of refining is going on?"

"Oh, yes ma'am," replied the silversmith, "I must sit and watch the furnace constantly, for, if the time necessary for refining is exceeded in the slightest degree, the silver will be injured."

The lady at once saw the beauty and comfort of the expression, "He shall sit as a refiner and

purifier of silver." God sees it necessary to put
His children into the furnace, but His eye is
steadily intent on the work of purifying, and His
wisdom and love are both engaged in the best
manner for us. Our trials do not come at random,
and He will not let us be tested beyond what we
can endure.

Before she left, the lady asked one final
question, "How do you know when the process
is complete?"

"That's quite simple," replied the silversmith.
"When I can see my own image in the silver, the
refining process is finished."

Today ...

_____

_____

_____

_____

_____

_____

_____

_____

_____

_____

Tomorrow ...

_____

_____

_____

_____

Write down your thoughts, dreams, and hopes.

*That the trial of your faith, being much
more precious than of gold that perisheth,
though it be tried with fire, might be found
unto praise and honour and glory at the
appearing of Jesus Christ.*

— I Peter 1:7

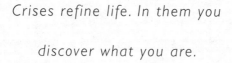

Crises refine life. In them you

discover what you are.

— Allan K. Chalmers

A few months ago, when I was picking up the children at school, another mother I knew well rushed up to me. Emily was fuming with indignation. "Do you know what you and I are?" she demanded. Before I could answer, and I didn't really have one handy, she blurted out the reason for her question. It seemed she had just returned from renewing her driver's license at the county clerk's office. Asked by the woman clerk to state her occupation. Emily had hesitated, uncertain how to classify herself. "What I mean is," explained the recorder, "Do you have a job, or are you just a — ?"

"Of course I have a job," snapped Emily. "I'm a mother."

"We don't list 'mother' as an occupation. 'Housewife' covers it," said the recorder emphatically.

I forgot all about her story until one day I

found myself in the same situation, this time at our own town hall. The clerk was obviously a career woman, poised, efficient, and probably possessed a high-sounding title like "official interrogator" or "town registrar."

"And what is your occupation?" she probed.

What made me say it, I do not know. The words simply popped out. "I'm a research associate in the field of child development and human relations."

The clerk paused, ballpoint pen frozen in midair, and looked up as though she had not heard right. I repeated the title slowly, emphasizing the most significant words. Then I stared with wonder as my pompous pronouncement was written in bold, black ink on the official questionnaire.

"Might I ask," said the clerk with new interest, "just what you do in your field?"

Coolly, without any trace of fluster in my voice, I heard myself reply, "I have a continuing program of research" (what mother doesn't) "in the laboratory and in the field" (normally I would have said indoors and out). "I'm working for my master's" (the whole family) "and already have four credits" (all daughters).

"Of course, the job is one of the most demanding in the humanities" (any mother care to disagree?) "and I often work 14 hours a day" (24 is more like it). "But the job is more challenging than most run-of-the-mill careers and the rewards are in satisfaction rather than just money."

There was an increasing note of respect in the clerk's voice as she completed the form, stood up, and personally ushered me to the door.

As I drove into our driveway, buoyed up by

my glamorous new career, I was greeted by my lab assistants, ages 13, 7, and 3. Upstairs I could hear our new experimental model (6 months) in the child-development program, testing out a new vocal pattern. I felt triumphant! I had scored a beat on bureaucracy! And I had gone on the official records as someone more distinguished and indispensable to mankind than "just another mother."

Motherhood ... what a glorious career. Especially when there's a title on the door.

TODAY...

_____
_____
_____
_____
_____
_____
_____
_____
_____
_____
_____

TOMORROW...

_____
_____
_____
_____

Write down your thoughts, dreams, and hopes.

> *She looks well to the ways of her household,*
> *and does not eat the bread of idleness.*
> — Proverbs 31:27 (RSV)

The most important occupation on earth for a woman is to be a real mother to her children. It does not have much glory to it; there is a lot of grit and grime. But there is no greater place of ministry, position, or power than that of a mother.

— Phil Whisenhunt

A WOMAN'S WORTH

John Cheever was asked if he would describe life with his wife, Mary. "She has displayed an extraordinary amount of patience," he answered. He paused, then continued, "Women are an inspiration. It's because of them we put on clean shirts and wash our necks. Because of women, we want to excel. Because of a woman, Christopher Columbus discovered America."

"Queen Isabella?" Mary Cheever murmured.

"I was thinking of Mrs. Columbus," he said, deadpan.

Many women have done excellently, but you surpass them all.
– Proverbs 31:29 (RSV)

TODAY ...

TOMORROW...

Write down your thoughts, dreams, and hopes.

THE SALARY

ob Greene (in the Detroit Free Press) cited a study by attorney Michael Minton on the monetary value of a wife's services in the home. First he listed the various functions she performs: chauffeur, gardener, family counselor, maintenance worker, cleaning woman, housekeeper, cook, errand runner, bookkeeper/budget manager, interior decorator, caterer, dietitian, secretary, public relations person, hostess. Using this impressive list of household duties, Minton figured the dollar value of a housewife's work in today's labor market. He came up with the amount of $785.07 a week. That's $40,823.64 a year!

Who can find a virtuous woman? for her price is far above rubies.
– Proverbs 31:10

T ODAY ...

_____

_____

_____

_____

_____

_____

_____

_____

_____

_____

T OMORROW ...

_____

_____

_____

_____

_____

Write down your thoughts, dreams, and hopes.

PROVERBS 31 WOMAN

B ishop Taylor came the closest of anyone
to capturing the sentiment of Proverbs 31
when he wrote: "If you are for pleasure, marry.
If you prize rosy health, marry. A good wife is
heaven's last best gift to a man; his angel of mercy;
minister of graces innumerable; his gem of many
virtues; his box of jewels; her voice, his sweetest
music; her smiles, his brightest day; her kiss, the
guardian of innocence; her arms, the pale of his
safety; the balm of his health; the balsam of his life;
her industry, his surest wealth; her economy, his
safest steward; her lips, his faithful counselors …
and her prayers, the ablest advocates of heaven's
blessing on his head." [1]

*The heart of her husband trusts in her, and
he will have no lack of gain.*
– Proverbs 31:11 (RSV)

TODAY ...

_____
_____
_____
_____
_____
_____
_____
_____
_____
_____
_____

TOMORROW ...

_____
_____
_____
_____

Write down your thoughts, dreams, and hopes.

THE SMARTEST CHILD

Y ou can have a brighter child, it all depends
on your expectations. Before you're tempted
to say, "Not true," let me tell you about Harvard
social psychologist Robert Rosenthal's classic
study. All the children in one San Francisco grade
school were given a standard I.Q. test at the
beginning of the school year. The teachers were
told the test could predict which students could
be expected to have a spurt of academic and
intellectual functioning. The researchers then
drew names out of a hat and told the teachers
that these were the children who had displayed
a high potential for improvement. Naturally, the
teachers thought they had been selected because
of their test performance and began treating
these children as special children.

And the most amazing thing happened
— the spurters, spurted! Overall, the "late
blooming" kids averaged four more I.Q. points on

the second test than the other group of students. However, the gains were most dramatic in the lowest grades. First graders whose teachers expected them to advance intellectually jumped 27.4 points, and the second grade spurters increased on the average 16.5 points more than their peers. One little Latin-American child who had been classified as mentally retarded with an I.Q. of 61, scored 106 after his selection as a late bloomer.

Isn't this impressive! It reminds me of what Eliza Doolittle says in *My Fair Lady*, "The difference between a lady and a flower girl is not how she behaves, but how she is treated." You see, how a child is treated has a lot to do with how that child sees herself and ultimately behaves. If a child is treated as a slow learner and you don't expect much, the child shrugs her shoulders and says, "Why should I try? Nobody thinks I can do it anyway!" And she gives up. But if you look at that child as someone who has more potential than she will ever be able to develop, you will challenge that child, work with her through discouragement, and find ways to explain concepts so the child can understand. You won't mind investing time in the child because you know your investment is going to pay off! And the result? It does!

So, what's the message for parents? Just this: Every child benefits from someone who believes in him, and the younger the child, the more important it is to have high expectations. You may not have an Einstein, but your child has possibilities! Expect the best and chances are, that's exactly what you'll get. [2]

> *For unto whomsoever much is given, of him shall be much required.*
>
> – Luke 12:48

TODAY ...

_____

_____

_____

_____

_____

_____

_____

_____

_____

_____

TOMORROW ...

_____

_____

_____

_____

Write down your thoughts, dreams, and hopes.

GIVING THANKS

Dear Lord,

Thank you for this child that I call mine; not my possession but my sacred charge. Teach me patience and humility so that the best I know may flow in its being. Let me always remember, parental love is my natural instinct but my child's love must ever be deserved and earned; that for love I must give love, that for understanding I must give understanding, that for respect, I must give respect; that as I was the giver of life, so must I be the giver always. Help me to share my child with life and not to clutch at it for my own sake. Give courage to do my share to make this world a better place for all children and my own.

For this child I prayed; and the LORD has granted me my petition which I made to him.
— 1 Samuel 1:27 (RSV)

TODAY...

_____
_____
_____
_____
_____
_____
_____
_____
_____
_____

TOMORROW...

_____
_____
_____
_____

Write down your thoughts, dreams, and hopes.

I LOVED YOU ENOUGH

Y ou don't love me!" How many times have your kids laid that one on you? Someday when my children are old enough to understand the logic motivation of a mother, I'll tell them:

I loved you enough to bug you about where you were going and what time you would get home.

I loved you enough to let you discover your friend was a creep.

I loved you enough to stand over you for two hours while you cleaned your bedroom, a job that would have taken me 15 minutes.

I loved you enough to ignore what every other mother did or said.

I loved you enough to let you stumble, fall, hurt, and fail.

I loved you enough to accept you for what you are, not what I wanted you to be.

Most of all, I loved you enough to say no when you hated me for it.

Some mothers don't know when their job is finished. They figure the longer the kids hang around, the better parents they are.

I see children as kites. You spend a lifetime trying to get them off the ground. You run with them until you're both breathless ... they crash ... you add a longer tail. You patch and comfort, adjust and teach — and assure them that someday they will fly.

Finally they are airborne, but they need more string, and you keep letting it out. With each twist of the ball of twine, the kite becomes more distant. You know it won't be long before that beautiful creature will snap the lifeline that bound you together and soar — free and alone. Only then do you know you did your job.[3]

T ODAY ...

T OMORROW ...

Write down your thoughts, dreams, and hopes.

> *Her children rise up and call her blessed;*
> *her husband also, and he praises her.*
> — Proverbs 31:28

The mother's heart is the

child's schoolroom.

— Henry Ward Beecher

A MOTHER'S KISS

Benjamin West was just trying to be a good babysitter for his little sister Sally. While his mother was out, Benjamin found some bottles of colored ink and proceeded to paint Sally's portrait. But by the time Mrs. West returned, ink blots stained the table, chairs, and floor. Benjamin's mother surveyed the mess without a word until she saw the picture. Picking it up, she exclaimed, "Why, it's Sally!" And she bent down and kissed her young son.

In 1763, when he was 25 years old, Benjamin West was selected as history painter to England's King George III. He became one of the most celebrated artists of his day.

Commenting on his start as an artist, he said, "My mother's kiss made me a painter." Her encouragement did far more than a rebuke ever could have done.[4]

> *And let us consider how to stir up one another to love and good works.*
> – Hebrews 10:24 (RSV)

TODAY...

_____

_____

_____

_____

_____

_____

_____

_____

TOMORROW...

_____

_____

_____

_____

Write down your thoughts, dreams, and hopes.

A MOTHER'S INFLUENCE

As a lawyer, as a congressman, as governor of Ohio, and as president of the United States, William McKinley had a close relationship with his mother. He either visited her or sent a message to her every day.

When she became seriously ill, he arranged to have a special train standing by, ready to take him to her bedside. Mrs. McKinley died December 12, 1897, in the arms of her 54-year-old son. Her gentle, Christian virtues helped mold the president's character, for when he was gunned down in Buffalo, New York, about four years later, he showed no bitterness toward his assassin. With Christian courage he said, "God's will be done." Before he died, he asked to hear once again the hymn "Nearer, My God, to Thee," which his mother had taught him.

Perhaps you too have been blessed with a Christian heritage. But unlike McKinley, you've strayed from God. On this day ... confess your sin and come back to the Lord. Let the precious memories of that special person in your life, who all these years has been pointing you to God, awaken in your heart a new desire to live for Him. Don't turn your back on the influence of your godly mother. [5]

Today ...

Tomorrow ...

Write down your thoughts, dreams, and hopes.

> I thank God . . . when I call to remembrance the genuine faith that is in you, which dwelt first in . . . your mother.
>
> — 2 Timothy 1:3,5

Blessed is the influence of

one true, loving human

soul on another.

— George Eliot

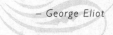

The relationship between a mother and daughter is unique. Whether it is good or bad, the one thing that remains constant is the connection between the two of them.

In *Psychology Today*, in the May/June 2001 issue, an article called "Enduring Love: The Mother-Daughter Connection Stays Strong Through Tough Times" stated that "88 percent of adults say their mother has had a positive influence on them, and 92 percent say their current relationship with their mother is positive." The article also states that, "There is a great value in the mother-daughter tie because the two parties care for one another and share a strong investment in the family as a whole, says Fingerman, author of *Aging Mothers and Their Daughters: A Study in Mixed Emotions* (Springer, 2001)."

As babies our mothers sat up all night when

we were sick. As school kids, our mothers made cupcakes for our class, and as teenage girls, we always went to our mothers for advice about boys, fashion, sex, menstrual cycle, and makeup. As mothers ourselves, we call our moms for child-care advice.

Our moms were always there to calm our dads down when we first started dating, our moms bought us our first bra, and they prepared us for womanhood.

No matter what age we are, our moms seem to have all the answers. They are the ones who brought us into this world, they are the ones that taught us about self-love, and our moms are the ones who love us unconditionally.

When I was in my teens, I had a friend who wasn't allowed to wear makeup; in fact, her father was dead set against it. But her mom went behind Dad's back and let her daughter wear the makeup as long as she took it off before her father got home. She was seventeen years old.

Some people may think that this is not right, going against your husband's beliefs, but this is why moms are special. They understand us daughters and they understand our needs.

Today let us celebrate motherhood and the relationships we have with our moms.

Take your mom out to lunch, grab an ice cream cone and be silly.

Make an appointment for manicures and pedicures together.

Go to a matinee and share a bucket of popcorn.

Rent some chick flicks and tear-jerking movies, and cuddle on the couch together.

Look at some old pictures of yourself growing up with your mom or watch some home movies.

Plant a rose bush and make a garden. Dedicate it to your mom.

Some of us live miles away from our parents, so e-mail an e-mail greeting card, postal mail a coupon stating that the next time you see her, a special event is being planned. Mother's Day should be celebrated all year round. It is never too late.

TODAY ...

TOMORROW ...

Write down your thoughts, dreams, and hopes.

> Honour thy father and thy mother: that thy days may be long upon the land which the LORD thy God giveth thee.
>
> – Exodus 20:12

Most of all the other beautiful things in life come by twos and threes by dozens and hundreds. Plenty of roses, stars, sunsets, rainbows, brothers and sisters, aunts and cousins, but only one mother in the whole world.

– Kate Douglas Wiggin

I Got Your Back...

I am a small and precious child, my dad's been
    sent to fight.
The only place I'll see his face, is in my dreams
    at night.
He will be gone too many days for my young
    mind to keep track.
I may be sad, but I am proud. My daddy's got
    your back.

I am a caring mother. My son has gone to war.
My mind is filled with worries that I have never
    known before.
Every day I try to keep my thoughts from
    turning black.
I may be scared, but I am proud. My son has
    got your back.

I am a strong and loving wife, with a husband
soon to go.
There are times I'm terrified in a way most
never know.
I bite my lip, and force a smile as I watch my
husband pack.
My heart may break, but I am proud. My
husband's got your back.

I am a soldier . . . serving proudly, standing tall.
I fight for freedom, yours and mine by answering
this call.
I do my job while knowing, the thanks it
sometimes lacks.
Say a prayer that I'll come home. It's me who's
got your back.[6]

T ODAY ...

T OMORROW ...

Write down your thoughts, dreams, and hopes.

Thou art my hiding place and my shield.
— Psalm 119:114

History does not long entrust

the care of freedom to the

weak or the timid.

— Dwight D. Eisenhower

THE MEANEST MOTHER

I had the meanest mother in the whole world. While other kids ate candy for breakfast, I had to have cereal, eggs, or toast. When others had Cokes and candy for lunch, I had to eat a sandwich. As you can guess, my supper was different than the other kids' also.

But at least, I wasn't alone in my sufferings. My sister and two brothers had the same mean mother as I did.

My mother insisted upon knowing where we were at all times. You'd think we were on a chain gang. She had to know who our friends were and where we were going. She insisted if we said we'd be gone an hour, that we be gone one hour or less — not one hour and one minute. I am nearly ashamed to admit it, but she actually struck us. Not once, but each time we had a mind of our own and did as we pleased. That poor belt was used more on our seats than it was to hold up Daddy's pants. Can you imagine someone actually hitting a child just because he disobeyed? Now you can begin to see how mean she really was.

We had to wear clean clothes and take a bath. The other kids always wore their clothes for days. We reached the height of insults because she made our clothes herself, just to save money. Why, oh why, did we have to have a mother who made us feel different from our friends?

The worst is yet to come. We had to be in bed by nine each night and up at eight the next morning. We couldn't sleep till noon like our friends. So while they slept, my mother actually had the nerve to break the child-labor law. She made us work. We had to wash dishes, make beds, learn to cook, and all sorts of cruel things. I believe she laid awake at night thinking up mean things to do to us.

She always insisted upon us telling the truth, the whole truth and nothing but the truth, even if it killed us — and it nearly did.

By the time we were teenagers, she was much wiser, and our life became even more unbearable. None of this tooting the horn of a car for us to come running. She embarrassed us to no end by making our dates and friends come to the door to get us. If I spent the night with a girlfriend, can you imagine — she checked on me to see if I was really there. I never had the chance to elope to Mexico. That is, if I'd had a boyfriend to elope with. I forgot to mention, while my friends were dating at the mature age of 12 and 13, my old-fashioned mother refused to let me date until the age of 15 and 16. Fifteen, that is, if I dated only to go to a school function. And that was maybe twice a year.

Through the years, things didn't improve a bit. We could not lie in bed "sick," like our friends did, and miss school. If our friends had a toe ache, a hangnail or serious ailment, they could stay home from school. Our marks in school had to be up to par. Our friends' report cards had beautiful colors on them, black for passing, red for failing. My mother, being as different as she was, would settle for nothing less than ugly black marks.

As the years rolled by, first one and then the other of us was put to shame. We were graduated from high school. With our mother behind us, talking, hitting and demanding respect, none of us was allowed the pleasure of being a drop-out.

My mother was a complete failure as a mother. Out of four children, a couple of us attained some higher education. None of us has ever been arrested, divorced, or has beaten his mate. Each of my brothers served his time in the service of this country. And whom do we have to blame for the terrible way we turned out? You're right, our mean mother. Look at the things we missed. We never got to march in a protest parade, nor take part in a riot, burn draft cards, and a million and one other things that our friends did. She forced us to grow up into God-fearing, educated, honest adults.

Using this as a background, I am trying to raise my three children. I stand a little taller and I am filled with pride when my children call me mean.

Because, you see, I thank God, He gave me the meanest mother in the whole world.[7]

T ODAY ...

T OMORROW ...

Write down your thoughts, dreams, and hopes.

> *He who ignores instruction despises himself, but he who heeds admonition gains understanding.*
> — Proverbs 15:32 (RSV)

No horse gets anywhere until he is harnessed. No steam or gas ever drives anything until it is confined. No Niagara is ever turned into light and power until it is tunneled. No life ever grows great until it is focused, dedicated, disciplined.

— Harry Fosdick

STAGES BY THE AGES

4 YEARS OF AGE

My Mommy can do anything!

8 YEARS OF AGE

My Mom knows a lot! A whole lot!

12 YEARS OF AGE

My Mother doesn't really know quite
everything.

14 YEARS OF AGE

Naturally, Mother doesn't know that either.

16 YEARS OF AGE

Mother? She's hopelessly old-fashioned.

18 YEARS OF AGE

That old woman? She's way out of date!

25 YEARS OF AGE

Well, she might know a little bit about it.

35 YEARS OF AGE

Before we decide, let's get Mom's opinion.

45 YEARS OF AGE

Wonder what Mom would have thought about it?

65 YEARS OF AGE

Wish I could talk it over with Mom once more . . .

TODAY ...

_____

_____

_____

_____

_____

_____

_____

_____

_____

_____

TOMORROW ...

_____

_____

_____

_____

Write down your thoughts, dreams, and hopes.

> *And thine age shall be clearer than the noonday; thou shalt shine forth, thou shalt be as the morning.*
>
> —Job 11:17

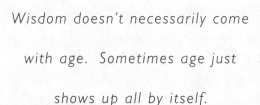

Wisdom doesn't necessarily come with age. Sometimes age just shows up all by itself.

— Tom Wilson

To My Child

J ust for this morning, I am going to smile when I see your face and laugh when I feel like crying.

Just for this morning, I will let you wake up softly, all rumpled in your sheets and I will hold you until you are ready for the day. Just for this morning, I will let you choose what you want to wear, and smile and say how perfect it is.

Just for this morning, I am going to step over the laundry, and pick you up and take you to the park to play.

Just for this morning, I will leave the dishes in the sink, and let you teach me how to put that puzzle of yours together.

Just for this afternoon, I will unplug the telephone and keep the computer off, and sit with you in the back yard and blow bubbles.

Just for this afternoon, I will not yell once, not even a tiny grumble when you scream and whine for the ice cream truck, and I will buy you one if he comes by.

Just for this afternoon, I won't worry about what you are going to be when you grow up, or second-guess every decision I have made where you are concerned.

Just for this afternoon, I will let you help me bake cookies, and I won't stand over you trying to fix them.

Just for this afternoon, I will take you to McDonald's and buy us both a Happy Meal so you can have both toys.

Just for this evening, I will hold you in my arms and tell you a story about when you were born, and how much I love you. Just for this evening, I will let you splash in the tub and not get angry.

Just for this evening, I will let you stay up late while we sit on the porch and count all the stars.

Just for this evening, I will snuggle beside you for hours, and miss my favorite TV show.

Just for this evening, when I run my fingers through your hair as you pray, I will simply be grateful that God has given me the greatest gift ever given. I will think about the mothers who are searching for their missing children, the mothers who are visiting their children's graves instead of their bedrooms, and mothers who are in hospital rooms watching their children suffer senselessly, and screaming inside that they can't handle it anymore, and when I kiss you goodnight I will hold you a little tighter, a little longer. It is then that I will thank God for you, and ask Him for nothing, except one more day.

$\mathbf{T}$ODAY ...

$\mathbf{T}$OMORROW ...

Write down your thoughts, dreams, and hopes.

> *Keep me as the apple of the eye; hide me in the shadow of thy wings.*
>
> – Psalm 17:8

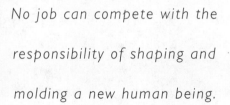

No job can compete with the

responsibility of shaping and

molding a new human being.

– James Dobson

A story is told that provides a penetrating picture of God's wings. After a forest fire in Yellowstone National Park, forest rangers began their trek up a mountain to assess the inferno's damage.

One ranger found a bird literally petrified in ashes, perched statuesquely on the ground at the base of a tree. Somewhat sickened by the eerie sight, he knocked over the bird with a stick. When he struck it, three tiny chicks scurried from under their dead mother's wings. The loving mother, keenly aware of impending disaster, had carried her offspring to the base of the tree and had gathered them under her wings, instinctively knowing that the toxic smoke would rise. She could have flown to safety but had refused to

abandon her babies. When the blaze had arrived
and the heat had singed her small body, the
mother had remained steadfast. Because she had
been willing to die, those under the cover of her
wings would live.

Kinda reminds you of what Jesus did for us!
Learn to experience the warmth and protection
of life beneath the wings of the Almighty.

Today ...

_____

_____

_____

_____

_____

_____

_____

_____

_____

_____

_____

Tomorrow ...

_____

_____

_____

_____

_____

Write down your thoughts, dreams, and hopes.

> *He shall cover thee with his feathers, and*
> *under his wings shalt thou trust.*
>
> — Psalm 91:4

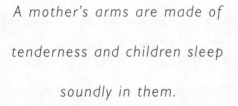

A mother's arms are made of

tenderness and children sleep

soundly in them.

— Victor Hugo

Clint's Song

For six years now, I've been the one to love you, teach you, my little son.

I've been there to repair the wounds, soothe your feelings and chase away the gloom.

But today you walk with lunchbox in hand, out the door, down the steps, all alone you will stand.

Waving goodbye, with tears in my eyes, I'll just pray that the world will treat you kind.

Here he is, teach him gently, his innocent eyes haven't seen the other side.

He thinks everyone loves him, he thinks everyone's kind.

Teachers please teach him gently, when he learns life isn't fair and all men are not true, he thinks you're a hero, he's depending on you.

I guess I've known this day would come, ready or not your journey's begun.

I want to freeze this moment, make a memory right now, while you think the world is your playground.

I wish that I could capture your spirit, lock it tight in a jar so I could always remember your childlike charm.

Waving goodbye, with tears in my eyes, I'll just pray that the world will treat you kind.

Bye Baby.

T ODAY ...

T OMORROW ...

Write down your thoughts, dreams, and hopes.

> Therefore also I have lent him to the LORD;
> as long as he liveth he shall be lent
> to the LORD.
>
> – I Samuel 1:28

The tie which links mother

and child is of such pure and

immaculate strength as to be

never violated.

Washington Irving

A QUICK RIDE HOME

A few months back, I stopped to pick up a few groceries after work. As we so often tend to run out of things during the middle of the week, a quick run is often vital. I made my purchases (more than I ran in for as usual) and proceeded to my car throwing the bags in the back seat.

I headed out of the parking lot and while driving slowly to the exit, I spotted this woman pushing a carriage loaded with groceries. She seemed to be using all her strength and I wondered where her car might be as she was close to the exit of the parking lot. Upon closer observation, not only was she pushing a full carriage but also a toddler was tucked in the seat. He looked about four. I glanced around again thinking maybe her car had broken down close by but no car was in sight. I came up close to her and rolled my window down asking her if she had far to go. . . . She spoke in broken English and said to the beach. I asked her if her car was close by and she replied she had no car and had missed the bus. *Well,* my heart said, *she can't do this alone; she needs some help.* I asked her if she would like a ride and I swear her eyes lit up with a big reply of, "Oh yes." I loaded the groceries in the trunk and put her and her son in the back buckled up close. She directed me out of the parking lot and although I did not understand her when she said the street name, I kept making rights and lefts.

She did mention she was from somewhere in or near Bosnia. We were now four or five miles from the shopping area. Finally, I understood the street name and recognized it as my husband's old neighborhood when he was a boy. Then as we went down the street, I also realized it was the same street where he spent his childhood. She pointed to a house and, would you believe, it was the same house he grew up in. Everything was almost the same. I pulled in the driveway, helped her unload the groceries, and her son came up to me and said, "Thank you for helping my mom."

The woman embraced me and said, "I prayed for an angel and God sent me you."

TODAY ...

_____

_____

_____

_____

_____

_____

_____

_____

_____

_____

_____

TOMORROW ...

_____

_____

_____

_____

Write down your thoughts, dreams, and hopes.

> *Be not forgetful to entertain strangers:*
> *for thereby some have entertained*
> *angels unawares.*
> — Hebrews 13:2

Successful people are always looking

for opportunities to help others.

Unsuccessful people are always

asking, "What's in it for me?"

— *Brian Tracy*

CAB DRIVER & ELDERLY LADY

Twenty years ago, I drove a cab for a living. It was a cowboy's life, a life for someone who wanted no boss. What I didn't realize was that it was also a ministry. Because I drove the night shift, my cab became a moving confessional. Passengers climbed in, sat behind me in total anonymity, and told me about their lives. I encountered people whose lives amazed me, ennobled me, made me laugh and weep. But none touched me more than a woman I picked up late one August night. I was responding to a call from a small brick fourplex in a quiet part of town.

I assumed I was being sent to pick up some partiers, or someone who had just had a fight with a lover, or a worker heading to an early shift at some factory in the industrial part of town.

When I arrived at 2:30 a.m., the building was dark except for a single light in a ground floor window. Under such circumstances, many drivers just honk once or twice, wait a minute, then drive away. But I had seen too many impoverished people who depended on taxis as their only means of transportation. Unless a situation smelled of danger, I always went to the door. *This passenger might be someone who needs my assistance,* I reasoned to myself. So I walked to the door and knocked.

"Just a minute," answered a frail, elderly voice. I could hear something being dragged across the floor. After a long pause, the door opened.

A small woman in her 80s stood before me. She was wearing a print dress and a pillbox hat with a veil pinned on it, like somebody out of a 1940s movie.

By her side was a small nylon suitcase. The apartment looked as if no one had lived in it for years. All the furniture was covered with sheets. There were no clocks on the walls, no knickknacks or utensils on the counters. In the corner was a cardboard box filled with photos and glassware.

"Would you carry my bag out to the car?"
she said. I took the suitcase to the cab, then
returned to assist the woman. She took my arm
and we walked slowly toward the curb. She kept
thanking me for my kindness. "It's nothing," I told
her. "I just try to treat my passengers the way I
would want my mother treated."

"Oh, you're such a good boy," she said.

When we got in the cab, she gave me an
address, then asked, "Can you drive through
downtown?"

"It's not the shortest way," I answered quickly.

"Oh, I don't mind," she said. "I'm in no hurry.
I'm on my way to a hospice." I looked in the
rearview mirror. Her eyes were glistening. "I don't
have any family left," she continued. "The doctor
says I don't have very long."

I quietly reached over and shut off the meter.
"What route would you like me to take?" I asked.
For the next two hours, we drove through the
city. She showed me the building where she had
once worked as an elevator operator. We drove
through the neighborhood where she and her

husband had lived when they were newlyweds. She had me pull up in front of a furniture warehouse that had once been a ballroom where she had gone dancing as a girl.

Sometimes she'd ask me to slow in front of a particular building or corner and would sit staring into the darkness, saying nothing. As the first hint of sun was creasing the horizon, she suddenly said, "I'm tired. Let's go now."

We drove in silence to the address she had given me. It was a low building, like a small convalescent home, with a driveway that passed under a portico.

Two orderlies came out to the cab as soon as we pulled up. They were solicitous and intent, watching her every move.

They must have been expecting her. I opened the trunk and took the small suitcase to the door. The woman was already seated in a wheelchair. "How much do I owe you?" she asked, reaching into her purse.

"Nothing," I said.

"You have to make a living," she answered.

"There are other passengers," I responded. Almost without thinking, I bent and gave her a hug. She held onto me tightly.

"You gave an old woman a little moment of joy," she said.

"Thank you." I squeezed her hand, then walked into the dim morning light. Behind me, a door shut. It was the sound of the closing of a life. I didn't pick up any more passengers that shift. I drove aimlessly, lost in thought. For the rest of that day, I could hardly talk. What if that woman had gotten an angry driver, or one who was impatient to end his shift? What if I had refused to take the run, or had honked once, then driven away? On a quick review, I don't think that I have done anything more important in my life. We're conditioned to think that our lives revolve around great moments. But great moments often catch us unaware, beautifully wrapped in what others may consider a small one.

TODAY ...

TOMORROW ...

Write down your thoughts, dreams, and hopes.

> *Be kindly affectioned one to another with brotherly love .... Distributing to the necessity of saints; given to hospitality.*
> — Romans 12:10-13

Character may be manifested in

the great moments, but it is made

in the small ones.

— Phillips Brooks

I t was one of the hottest days of the dry
season. We had not seen rain in almost a
month. The crops were dying. Cows had stopped
giving milk. The creeks and streams were long
gone back into the earth. It was a dry season that
would bankrupt several farmers before it was
through.

Every day, my husband and his brothers
would go about the arduous process of trying
to get water to the fields. Lately this process
had involved taking a truck to the local water
rendering plant and filling it up with water. But
severe rationing had cut everyone off. If we didn't
see some rain soon . . . we would lose everything.

It was on this day that I learned the true
lesson of sharing and witnessed the only miracle I
have seen with my own eyes. I was in the kitchen
making lunch for my husband and his brothers
when I saw my six-year-old son, Billy, walking
toward the woods. He wasn't walking with the
usual carefree abandon of a youth but with a

serious purpose. I could only see his back. He was obviously walking with a great effort ... trying to be as still as possible.

Minutes after he disappeared into the woods, he came running out again, toward the house. I went back to making sandwiches; thinking that whatever task he had been doing was completed. Moments later, however, he was once again walking in that slow purposeful stride toward the woods. This activity went on for an hour: walk carefully to the woods, run back to the house. Finally I couldn't take it any longer and I crept out of the house and followed him on his journey (being very careful not to be seen ... as he was obviously doing important work and didn't need his mommy checking up on him). He was cupping both hands in front of him as he walked; being very careful not to spill the water he held in them.... Maybe two or three tablespoons were held in his tiny hands. I sneaked close as he went into the woods.

Branches and thorns slapped his little face but he did not try to avoid them. He had a much higher purpose. As I leaned in to spy on him, I saw the most amazing sight. Several large deer loomed in front of him. Billy walked right up to them. I almost screamed for him to get away. A huge buck with elaborate antlers was dangerously close. But the buck did not threaten him. . . . He didn't even move as Billy knelt down. And I saw a tiny fawn laying on the ground, obviously suffering from dehydration and heat exhaustion, lift its head with great effort to lap up the water cupped in my beautiful boy's hand. When the water was gone, Billy jumped up to run back to the house and I hid behind a tree.

I followed him back to the house; to a spigot that we had shut off the water to. Billy opened it all the way up and a small trickle began to creep out. He knelt there, letting the drip, drip slowly fill up his makeshift "cup," as the sun beat down on his little back. And it came clear to me. The trouble he had gotten into for playing with the hose the week before. The lecture he had received about the importance of not wasting water. The reason he didn't ask me to help him.

It took almost twenty minutes for the drops to fill his hands. When he stood up and began the trek back, I was there in front of him. His little eyes just filled with tears. "I'm not wasting," was all he said. As he began his walk, I joined him ... with a small pot of water from the kitchen. I let him tend to the fawn. I stayed away. It was his job. I stood on the edge of the woods watching the most beautiful heart I have ever known working so hard to save another life. As the tears that rolled down my face began to hit the ground, they were suddenly joined by other drops ... and more drops ... and more. I looked up at the sky. It was as if God, himself, was weeping with pride.

Some will probably say that this was all just a huge coincidence. That miracles don't really exist. That it was bound to rain sometime. And I can't argue with that. ... I'm not going to try. All I can say is that the rain that came that day saved our farm ... just like the actions of one little boy saved another. I don't know if anyone will read this ... but I had to send it out. To honor the memory of my beautiful Billy, who was taken from me much too soon. ... But not before showing me the true face of God, in a little sunburned body.

TODAY ...

TOMORROW ...

Write down your thoughts, dreams, and hopes.

> Greater love hath no man than this, that a
> man lay down his life for his friends.
> — John 15:13

We cannot tell the precise moment

when friendship formed. As in filling a

vessel drop by drop, there is at last a

drop which makes it run over; so in a

series of kindness there is at last one

which makes the heart run over.

— Dr. Samuel Johnson

SAYING THE BLESSING

A woman invited some people to dinner. At the table, she turned to her six-year-old daughter and said, "Would you like to say the blessing?"

"I wouldn't know what to say," the little girl replied.

"Just say what you hear Mommy say," the mother said.

The little girl bowed her head and said, "Dear Lord, why on earth did I invite all these people to dinner?" [8]

Children seldom misquote. In fact,

they usually repeat word for word

what you shouldn't have said.

– Anonymous

Today ...

_____

_____

_____

_____

_____

_____

_____

_____

_____

_____

Tomorrow ...

_____

_____

_____

_____

_____

Write down your thoughts, dreams, and hopes.

GIFTS THAT DO NOT COST A CENT

THE GIFT OF LISTENING ...

But you must REALLY listen.

No interrupting, no daydreaming, no planning
your response. Just listening.

THE GIFT OF AFFECTION ...

Be generous with appropriate hugs, kisses,
pats on the back and handholds.

Let these small actions demonstrate the love
you have for family and friends.

THE GIFT OF LAUGHTER ...

Clip cartoons.

Share articles and funny stories.

Your gift will say, "I love to laugh with you."

THE GIFT OF A WRITTEN NOTE ...

    It can be a simple "Thanks for the help"
        note or a full sonnet.
    A brief, handwritten note may be
        remembered for a lifetime, and may
        even change a life.

THE GIFT OF A COMPLIMENT ...

    A simple and sincere, "You look great in
        red," "You did a super job or "That
        was a wonderful meal," can make
        someone's day.

THE GIFT OF A FAVOR ...

    Every day, go out of your way to do
        something kind.

THE GIFT OF SOLITUDE ...

There are times when we want nothing
better than to be left alone.

Be sensitive to those times and give the gift of
solitude to others.

THE GIFT OF A CHEERFUL DISPOSITION ...

The easiest way to feel good is to extend a
kind word to someone, really it's not that
hard to say hello or thank you.

Friends are a very rare jewel, indeed. They
make you smile and encourage you to
succeed. They lend an ear, they share a
word of praise, and they always want
to open their hearts to us. Show your
friends how much you care.[9]

TODAY ...

TOMORROW ...

Write down your thoughts, dreams, and hopes.

Even so by the righteousness of one the free gift came upon all men unto justification of life.

– Romans 5:18

I feel the greatest gift you can

give anyone is your honest self.

It's the only unique gift anyone

can give.

– Fred Rogers

THE CROSS ROOM

A young man was at the end of his rope. Seeing no way out, he dropped to his knees in prayer. "Lord, I can't go on," he said. "I have too heavy a cross to bear."

The Lord replied, "My son, if you can't bear its weight, just place your cross inside this room. Then open that other door and pick out any cross you wish."

The young man was filled with relief. "Thank you, Lord," he sighed, and he did what he was told. Upon entering the other door, he saw many other crosses, some so large the tops weren't even visible. Then he spotted a tiny cross leaning against the far wall. "I'd like that one Lord," he whispered.

And the Lord replied, "My son, that is the cross you just brought in."

Cast thy burden upon the LORD, and he shall sustain thee: he shall never suffer the righteous to be moved.

– Psalm 55:22

TODAY ...

TOMORROW ...

Write down your thoughts, dreams, and hopes.

I would have talked less and listened more.

I would have invited friends over to dinner even if the carpet was stained and the sofa faded.

I would have eaten the popcorn in the "good" living room and worried much less about the dirt when someone wanted to light a fire in the fireplace.

I would have taken the time to listen to my grandfather ramble about his youth.

I would never have insisted the car windows be rolled up on a summer day because my hair had just been teased and sprayed.

I would have burned the pink candle sculpted like a rose before it melted in storage.

I would have sat on the lawn with my children
and not worried about grass stains.

I would have cried and laughed less while
watching television — and more while
watching life.

I would have shared more of the responsibility
carried by my husband.

I would have gone to bed when I was sick instead
of pretending the earth would go into a
holding pattern if I weren't there for the day.

I would never have bought anything just because
it was practical, didn't show soil, or was
guaranteed to last a lifetime.

Instead of wishing away nine months of pregnancy, I'd have cherished every moment and realized that the wonderment growing inside me was the only chance in life to assist God in a miracle.

When my kids kissed me impetuously, I would never have said, "Later. Now go get washed up for dinner."

There would have been more "I love you's" ... more "I'm sorry's" ... but mostly, given another shot at life, I would seize every minute ... look at it and really see it ... live it ... and never give it back.[10]

TODAY ...

_____

_____

_____

_____

_____

_____

_____

_____

_____

_____

_____

TOMORROW ...

_____

_____

_____

_____

_____

Write down your thoughts, dreams, and hopes.

Let us hear the conclusion of the whole matter:
Fear God, and keep his commandments: for
this is the whole duty of man.

– Ecclesiastes 12:13

If I had my life to live over again,

I'd dare to make more mistakes

the next time.

– Nadine Stair

WELCOME TO HOLLAND

I am often asked to describe the experience
of raising a child with a disability, to try to
help people who haven't shared that unique
experience to understand it, to imagine how it
would feel. It's like this. . . .

When you're going to have a baby, it's like
planning a fabulous vacation trip to Italy. You buy
a bunch of guidebooks and make your wonderful
plans . . . the Coliseum, the Michelangelo,
gondolas. You may learn some handy phrases in
Italian. It's all very exciting.

After several months of eager anticipation,
the day finally arrives. You pack your bags and
off you go. Several hours later, the plane lands.
The stewardess comes in and says, "Welcome to
Holland."

"Holland?" you say. "What do you mean
Holland? I signed up for Italy! I'm supposed to be

in Italy. All my life I've dreamed of going to Italy."

But there's been a change in the flight plan. They've landed in Holland and there you must stay. The important thing is that they haven't taken you to a horrible, disgusting, filthy place full of pestilence, famine, and disease. It's just a different pace.

So you go out and buy new guidebooks and you must learn a whole new language and you will meet a whole new group of people you would have never met. It's just a different place. It's slower-paced than Italy, less flashy than Italy. But after you've been there for a while and you catch your breath, you look around. You begin to notice that Holland has windmills, Holland has tulips, and Holland even has Rembrandts.

But everyone you know is busy coming and going from Italy, and they're all bragging about what a wonderful time they had there. And for the rest of your life you will say, "Yes, that's where I was supposed to go. That's what I had planned." And the pain of that experience will never, ever, ever go away. The loss of that dream is a very significant loss.

But if you spend your life mourning the fact that you didn't get to Italy, you may never be free to enjoy the very special, the very lovely things about Holland.[11]

TODAY...

TOMORROW...

Write down your thoughts, dreams, and hopes.

We then that are strong ought to bear the infirmities of the weak, and not to please ourselves.

– Romans 15:1

When we lose one blessing,

another is often, most

unexpectedly, given in its place.

– C. S. Lewis

MAMA

Out shopping, my friend Darin noticed a mother with three little girls and a baby. The woman's patience was wearing thin as all the girls called "Mama" while she tried to shop.

Finally, Darin heard her say, "I don't want to hear the word MAMA for at least five minutes."

A few seconds went by, then one girl tugged on her mom's skirt and said, "Excuse me, miss." [12]

Knowing this, that the trying of your faith worketh patience. But let patience have her perfect work, that ye may be perfect and entire, wanting nothing.

— James 1:3-4

TODAY ...

TOMORROW ...

Write down your thoughts, dreams, and hopes.

References

[1] *Today in the Word*, July, 1989, p. 44.

[2] Kay Kuzma, *Family Times*, Vol. 1, No. 3, Fall, 1992, p. 1.

[3] Erma Bombeck, from "Forever, Erma," quoted in *Reader's Digest*, March 1997, p. 148.

[4] *Our Daily Bread*, March-May, 1996

[5] DJD, *Our Daily Bread*, May 14, 1995.

[6] Autumn Parker, *A Soldier's Bride*.

[7] Bobbie Pingaro.

[8] *Bits and Pieces*.

[9] *Bits and Pieces*.

[10] Erma Bombeck.

[11] Emily Kingsley (from anchoredbygrace.com).

[12] Mariel Raechal in *Reader's Digest*.

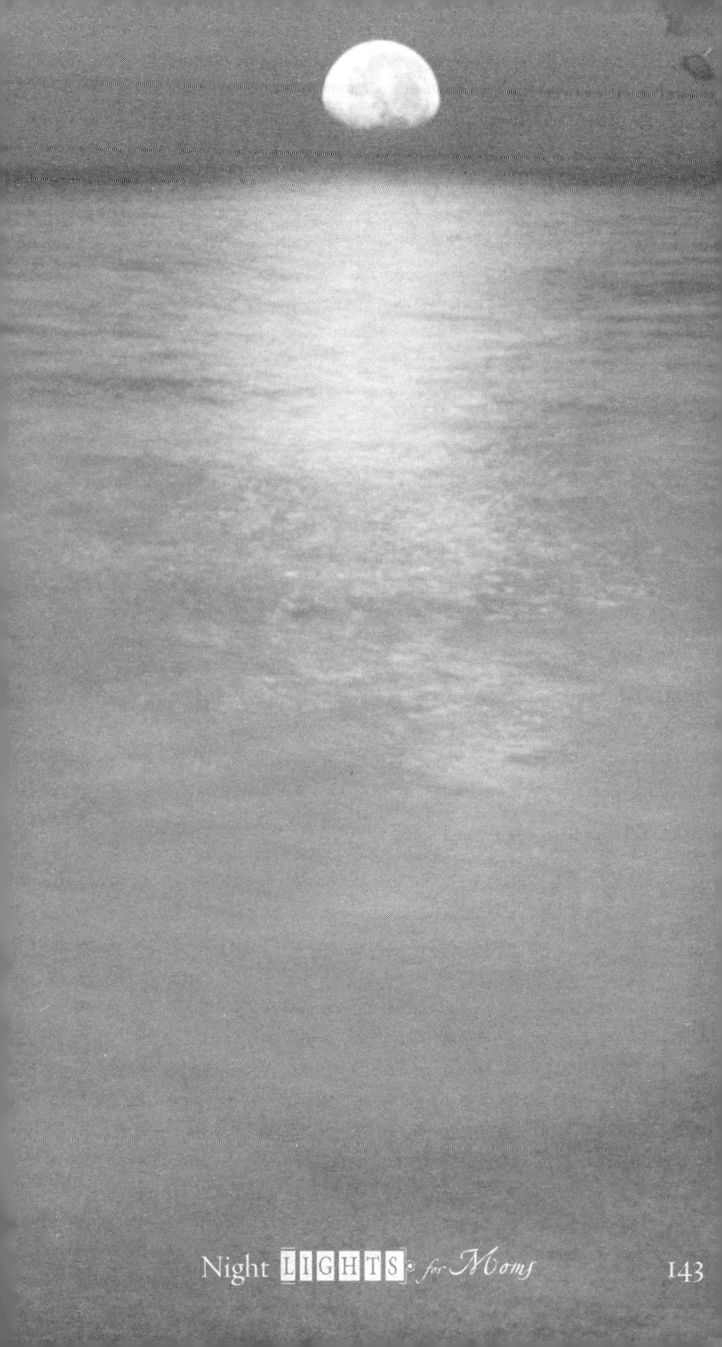

PHOTO CREDITS